This book is dedicated to my brother, Dr. Thomas Spier.

Other books by Peter Spier

The Fox Went Out on a Chilly Night
London Bridge Is Falling Down!
To Market! To Market!
Hurrah, We're Outward Bound!
And So My Garden Grows
Of Dikes and Windmills
The Erie Canal
Gobble, Growl, Grunt
Crash! Bang! Boom!
Fast-slow, High-low
The Star-Spangled Banner

TIN LIZZIE

TIN LIZZIE

Written and illustrated by Peter Spier

Doubleday & Company, Inc., Garden City, New York

SUMMARY: Chronicles the experiences of a Model T Ford with a series of owners from 1909 to the present day. [1. Automobiles—Fiction]
I. Title. ISBN 0-385-09470-1 Trade. 0-385-07069-1 Prebound. Library of Congress Catalog Card Number 74-1510. PZ7.S544Ti [Fic]
Copyright © 1975 by Peter Spier. All Rights Reserved. Printed in the United States of America. First Printing.

In the year 1909 the streets, highways, and country roads of our world looked very different from the way they look today. But things were beginning to change.

Many people—and not only the older ones—could well remember the days when bicycles (funny things called "velocipedes" with a huge front wheel and a small one right behind it) were a curious new invention.

"Just look at that daredevil," they would say. "Sooner or later he's bound to break his neck!"

But by now bicycles were so common a sight—even women were riding them—that not even dogs paid much attention to them any longer.

The horse reigned supreme. In the city they pulled trolleys over their rails. Horse-drawn cabs were the taxis of the day, and teams of huge draught horses pulled freight wagons everywhere. Doctors made their house calls in horse-drawn runabouts. Fire engines were pulled by horses, as were bakers' wagons and those of all the other tradesmen. And then, of course, there were the countless carriages that came in all shapes and sizes and bore strange names: Broughams, Landaulets, Phaetons, Roof-seat breaks, Victorias—and many more. In fact, the city streets were so choked with horse-drawn traffic that people used to say, "Goodness knows where it is all going to end."

In the country, too, horses did most of the work, pulling plows, cultivators, and harvesters, not to mention the farmers in their

surreys, buckboards, traps, and country wagons.

And all over the land tracks were built for the "iron horse."

But times were beginning to change for here and there you might see a strange motor-driven vehicle: the first "horseless carriages." They made a racket and were smelly, scaring horses and passers-by alike. But more and more of them appeared on the streets, and everybody got used to them. Even the horses.

Still, people who knew said seriously, "Mark my words, these new-fangled machines won't last. They're just a passing fad. Nothing will ever replace a good horse!"

But the new machines did not disappear. On the contrary, they multiplied, and in ever-increasing numbers, they could be seen and heard roaring along.

$10 FINE FOR DRIVING HORSES, CATTLE & MULES ON THIS BRIDGE FASTER THAN A WALK!

Early in May a brand new Model T touring car—the world would know it as a Tin Lizzie—rolled out of a great factory in Detroit. It was not the only one made, for on that same day fifty-six other Model Ts were built.

They were carefully tested and then driven to the parking lot behind the factory. The following day the cars were loaded aboard a long freight train. That afternoon most of the boxcars were left in a Chicago freight yard, but some were hooked up to another train that moved farther west. Before long, the boxcars arrived in a small midwestern town. The local dealer was waiting at the sid-

ing, and once his two cars had been unloaded and tied one behind the other, a team of horses slowly pulled them over the old, rutted dirt road into town, coming to a halt in front of his establishment, where a small crowd quickly assembled.

They were the first cars in town, and during the next few days just about every man and boy around came to inspect and admire them.

Even after the showroom closed, late-comers were still elbowing their way through the crowd in front of the windows for a long look at those shining cars.

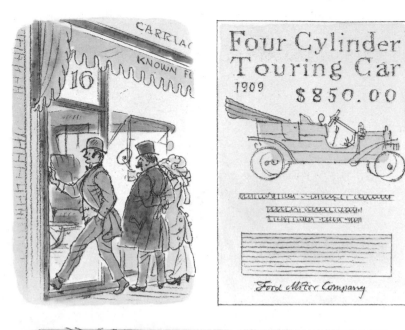

Among the first to see the automobiles was George Barnhart who owned the feed store. He not only came in the morning, but returned after lunch and once more later in the afternoon. On his way home from work he passed there again!

"Wouldn't be a bit surprised if George bought a machine tomorrow," the car dealer said to his wife that evening. "He came by at least four times today."

At roughly the same time Barnhart told his wife of "that dandy automobile" he just happened to catch a glimpse of that day, and the next morning the whole family trooped down to the showroom. Mr. Ferris did not have much of a selling job to do, but he did say, ". . . a great machine, yessir. Twenty horsepower, and she'll do every bit of forty-eight miles on the open road! Get behind the wheel, George, you too, Mary. Get the feel of it!"

In the meantime, the Barnhart children climbed all over both cars, touching everything they had been told not to.

The Barnharts bought the car and returned that afternoon to pick it up. It took the dealer only the better part of an hour to teach Mr. Barnhart how to operate Tin Lizzie.

The feed store owner did not get much work done that day: He drove his family all over town, past his father's house, past his store and even to the nearby farm of his in-laws. Wherever they went, people stopped to stare. "Look at that car," they said, "just look at that great new car!"

Some horses were scared, a few reared and shied, and Bob Swenson, the farmer, had to run out of the haberdashery in the new coat he was trying on, to calm his team.

Followed by running boys and dogs the Barnharts made one final stop at the drugstore to order a supply of gasoline, for in those days, there were no service stations.

"I'll have some bottles for you the day after tomorrow," said the druggist.

When they came home, Barnhart and his children pulled their surrey out of the stable and carefully backed Tin Lizzie inside. Their horse watched nervously from her stall, the whites of her eyes showing and her nostrils quivering at that strange odor of lacquer, gas, and oil which now mingled with the familiar stable smells of hay, leather, and horse.

The neighbors came for a look that evening for it was the first car in town! But not for long, because Dr. Garvin bought the other one two days later.

Happy days followed. George Barnhart still used his horse and buggy around town, but he used the car more and more for visiting on Sundays, for pleasure trips to the country, or for an occasional business trip to the city.

Tin Lizzie was well cared for. Her brass was kept immaculately polished and Mr. Barnhart often went to the stable to buff the hood even when it was not really called for.

Some problems occurred once in a while—tires were punctured by horse shoe nails, or a speck of dirt lodged in the carburetor. And there was that time when the engine quit six miles out of town. George Barnhart had to walk all the way home to get his

horse. Old Lucy towed them back to town, Barnhart steering, his wife holding the reins, and the children asleep in the back.

The roads were improved greatly as the years went by, and later the Barnharts could hardly remember the times when Lizzie had gotten stuck in the mud, or the scare they had had (it must have been in '16) when a bridge half collapsed as they passed over it.

Life was good. The children grew up and the two oldest were, in time, allowed to drive Lizzie, who had become as much a member of the family as old Lucy had once been.

Inevitably the day came when Mr. Barnhart said to his wife, "Mary, I saw a dandy new car at the agency today," (he really had been looking at it for weeks). "Electric self-starter, electric lights . . ."

And so Tin Lizzie—who was eleven years old and had traveled over 38,000 miles—was traded in for a brand new car.

The dealer fixed her up, gave her a set of new tires, waxed and polished her till she gleamed like new, and put her in his used-car lot.

Several people came to look at her. They kicked her tires and slammed the doors. "Sound as a bell," praised the young salesman. "You couldn't find a better car at that price anywhere." Which was true. "Come to think of it, I sold this car in 1909 to the original owner!" Which was not.

Lizzie stood there for several weeks until she was finally bought by a young couple about to be married. "Think of it," they said happily to each other as they drove away, "our first car!" The year was 1920 and no one turned his head to watch as Tin Lizzie drove by, for by now there were nearly as many cars as horses on the road.

The young couple were married and lavished every bit as much care and attention on their car as George Barnhart had, years ago. As a matter of fact, Lizzie saw parts of the world she did not even know existed because the young man found work far away from the small midwestern town. Tin Lizzie was driven through the plains, across mountains and rivers—all the way to California. She did her work well. "Best car we've ever owned," said the young couple time and again, forgetting that they had never owned another.

There were, to be sure, some small problems, such as the time when she was hit by a truck. Then, too, some parts had to be replaced occasionally, but that was to be expected.

Now that there were very few horses left on the road losing horseshoe nails, Tin Lizzie had only a few flat tires. These were happy years indeed. She took the young people on vacations, on short outings, and to work day after day. And one day she was driven at top speed to the hospital to take the young man's wife. Then, several days later they went back to pick her up—and the new baby as well! And, believe it or not, this happened three more times over the next six years!

The family moved back East, and in 1929 the young man (well, he was not so young any longer) decided that the time had come to get a new car. And so, for the second time in her life Lizzie ended up in the lot of a used-car dealer. She required a bit more fixing up this time. Some dents had to be taken out, and she was given a dab of paint here and there to hide a spot of rust. Her brass was polished again and she looked quite respectable, although there was no denying that she was no longer a young lady.

Times were hard in 1929, and there were many lookers but few buyers. As a result, Lizzie stood in the lot for almost a whole year, but was finally sold to a farmer for a small sum.

Her life was different now: No more picnics in the country or trips just for the fun of it, but hard work. Carrying milk cans back to the farm from distant fields, pulling wagons loaded with mountains of hay, and hauling others loaded with manure.

She did it all faithfully and willingly enough, and visitors to the farm would often remark, "That's a good machine you got yourself that time, neighbor. It sure doesn't owe you much by now!" And right they were.

On and on toiled Tin Lizzie. She was beginning to show her age and the signs of the rough work. The rear seats had been taken out long ago, and the stuffing of the front seat was showing through the torn leather. Her windshield was broken and one of her lamps hung at a sad angle.

It is almost unbelievable that she lasted as long as she did: thirty-six years in all! Late in 1945, Tin Lizzie was finally retired behind the barn next to an ancient plow and a broken, rusting rake. There was no way of telling how many miles she had traveled since her mileage meter had broken ages ago.

This, then, seemed to be the end—but not quite, for the farmer's children often came to see her, and played in and around the car, sitting behind the wheel pretending to take long journeys. Before long they outgrew that sort of thing and Lizzie was almost forgotten. At times a neighbor would come to "borrow" some parts of the old car, for many of them still had Model Ts of their own.

The weeds around Lizzie grew taller, and woodbine made its way through an open door, winding its shoots around the steering column and the tarnished levers. A maple seed was blown under the car, germinated there and the sapling grew up slowly past the engine, and in time through the open hood, well above the windshield.

In spring little twigs and wild flowers pushed out of the earth and mysteriously found their way through cracks in the floor boards. Honeysuckle wove itself playfully between the now almost paintless wooden spokes of the wheels. And one year a pair of small birds built a nest, precariously balanced, on some wires hidden underneath the dashboard.

After the hot summer, autumn would arrive and leaves from the trees around would fall and be blown into Lizzie, forming a fresh layer on top of others from falls long past. The snows would come and Tin Lizzie would appear just a black, rusty shape in all that whiteness. Mice and a stray raccoon might seek shelter inside if the winter was unusually harsh. Each spring after the last snow had melted and the earth was warming and greening again, there was a bit more rust on Lizzie, a few more rips and tears in her top, and a crack in the windshield that had not been there the previous year. Nothing else ever changed. And yet, some things had: There were no horses left on the farm; their work was now done by a tractor. Also, the shapes and colors of passing cars were different each year.

One day, many machines came from over the hills: bulldozers, scrapers, and earth-movers, building a great new road that passed quite near the farm. The old dirt road was still there, of course, and crossed under the new viaduct of the superhighway. Things were never the same again. It was no longer quiet there, with the continuous roar of trailer trucks, cars, and busses thundering by.

Not long afterward a curious procession moved past the farm: thirty-four old cars, on their way to an antique car rally. They all shone and sparkled like new, and their sputtering engines would have sounded very familiar to Lizzie had she been able to hear at all. The driver of one of those old cars—he must have had unusually keen eyes—spotted the familiar shape half hidden by weeds, behind the barn of the farm he was just then passing, and he made a mental note of the exact location of his discovery.

The following weekend he returned, and after looking Tin Lizzie over, knocked on the front door of the farm and asked Mr. Mogensen if he "would by any chance be interested in selling that old piece of rust behind the barn."

"Hmmm," that shrewd old farmer said. "I might, and then again, I might not. Pile of rust you say? Pile of rust? That, sir, is a 1909 Model T touring car, and not in bad shape at that!" Now that last statement was an outrageous lie, and they both knew it. In any case, the long and the short of it was that Mr. Mogensen sold Tin Lizzie then and there. A few days later Lizzie's new owner

came to fetch her, and with the farmer loaded the old car on the trailer, throwing bits and pieces belonging to Lizzie inside her.

The most amazing thing about it all was that Mr. Mogensen actually received much more money for Tin Lizzie than he had paid for her over forty years earlier. The most surprised man was the old fellow himself.

"I'll be hanged," he said to his wife, "what in the name of Heaven is he going to do with that pile of rust? You wouldn't think that anyone in his right mind would have given a penny for it. . . . Well, as they say, there's a fool born every day!"

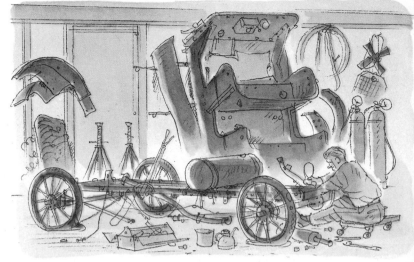

But that man was no fool at all. Far from it. He was a successful businessman, and a skilled amateur mechanic as well, who loved old cars, and over the next two-and-a-half years he lovingly restored Lizzie. He hunted all over the country for parts that were missing, and he painstakingly rebuilt the engine and the body. It was not an easy job—and not cheap either!

The neighbors often came to have a look at how things were progressing. It was like old times. Finally the day arrived when Lizzie was moved out of the garage, and there she stood reborn, shimmering in the sunlight, exactly the way she had looked on the day she was built. Maybe even better: her brass had never been polished brighter, her seven coats of lacquer had been buffed to perfection, and the windshield was like a mirror.

The man who had wrought this small miracle did not say much. He just walked around the car with his wife, a smile on his face, and looked perfectly happy. Just as happy as George Barnhart had been over half a century before . . .

On beautiful weekends Tin Lizzie is taken out on the road again for drives in the country—you might even see her someday on picnics, and to antique car meets. She can, of course, not go nearly as fast as the other cars on the road, but she gets where she is going just the same. The people in those new cars even slow down when they pass and turn their heads. The children will always say: "Wow, Dad! Did you see that old car?" And then their fathers invariably answer: "Sure did. When I was a boy my grandfather used to have one just like it," and they will smile at the memory.

In the city, too, a small crowd always quickly gathers around Lizzie when she is parked somewhere, just to look, and wherever she goes people will stop and say, "Oh, look at that car, just look at that great old car!"

1909 Ford Model T Touring Car

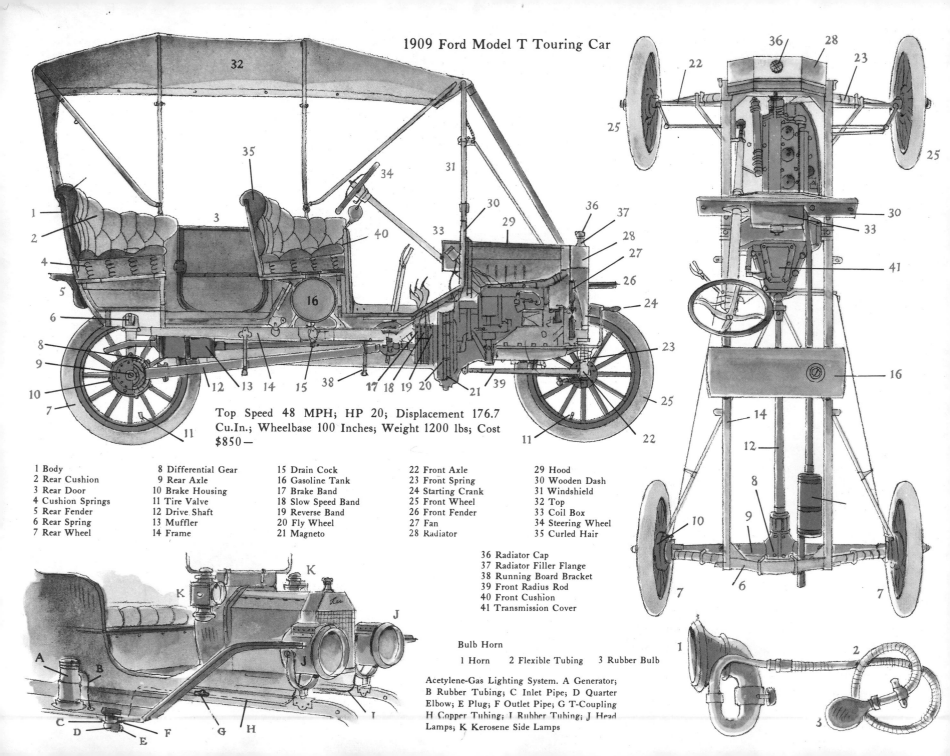

Top Speed 48 MPH; HP 20; Displacement 176.7
Cu.In.; Wheelbase 100 Inches; Weight 1200 lbs; Cost
$850 —

1 Body
2 Rear Cushion
3 Rear Door
4 Cushion Springs
5 Rear Fender
6 Rear Spring
7 Rear Wheel

8 Differential Gear
9 Rear Axle
10 Brake Housing
11 Tire Valve
12 Drive Shaft
13 Muffler
14 Frame

15 Drain Cock
16 Gasoline Tank
17 Brake Band
18 Slow Speed Band
19 Reverse Band
20 Fly Wheel
21 Magneto

22 Front Axle
23 Front Spring
24 Starting Crank
25 Front Wheel
26 Front Fender
27 Fan
28 Radiator

29 Hood
30 Wooden Dash
31 Windshield
32 Top
33 Coil Box
34 Steering Wheel
35 Curled Hair

36 Radiator Cap
37 Radiator Filler Flange
38 Running Board Bracket
39 Front Radius Rod
40 Front Cushion
41 Transmission Cover

Bulb Horn

1 Horn   2 Flexible Tubing   3 Rubber Bulb

Acetylene-Gas Lighting System. A Generator;
B Rubber Tubing; C Inlet Pipe; D Quarter
Elbow; E Plug; F Outlet Pipe; G T-Coupling
H Copper Tubing; I Rubber Tubing; J Head
Lamps; K Kerosene Side Lamps

Control System
1 Steering Wheel
2 Throttle 3 Switch
4 Emergency Brake and
Clutch Release 5 High
and Slow Speed Clutch
6 Reverse 7 Foot Brake
8 Gasoline Adjustment
9 Speedometer

A. 1 Spark Lever; 2 Throttle Lever; 3 Steering Gear Internal Gear Case; 4 Steering Gear Pinions Pin; 5 Top of Steering Post; 6 Throttle Quadrant; 7 Steering Gear Pinions; 8 Spark Quadrant; 9 Steering Gear Drive Pinion.

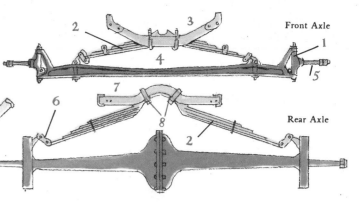

Front Axle

Rear Axle

1 Steering Knuckle; 2 Spring; 3 Frame Member; 4 Axle; 5 Steering Spindle; 6 Shackle; 7 Frame; 8 Spring Clips

B. 1 Steering Wheel; 2 Wheel Nut; 3 Throttle Lever; 4 Quadrant; 5 Steering Gear Case; 6 Spark Lever; 7 Steering Gear Spider.

The Engine and Transmission Unit. 1 Reverse Pedal; 2 Brake Pedal; 3 High and Slow Pedal; 4 Transmission Gears; 5 Magnets; 6 Magneto Coil; 7 Primary Contact; 8 Cylinder Head; 9 Piston; 10 Connecting Rod; 11 Piston Ring; 12 Water Jacket; 13 Top Water Connection; 14 Valve; 15 Exhaust Pipe; 16 Intake Pipe; 17 Valve Cover; 18 Breather Pipe 19 Fan; 20 Commutator; 21 Cylinder Casting; 22 Valve Spring; 23 Valve Stem; 24 Camshaft; 25 Push Rod; 26 Crank Shaft; 27 Crank Shaft Bearing; 28 Crank Case Oil Plug; 29 Crank Case Drain Cocks; 30 Transmission Shaft; 31 Crank Case; 32 Clutch Lever Shaft; 33 Clutch Finger; 34 Transmission Band; 35 Transmission Cover Door.

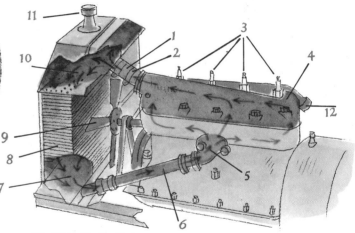

The Water Cooling System.

1 Top Hose; 2 Outlet Connection; 3 Spark Plugs; 4 Cylinder Head and Water Jackets; 5 Side Water Connection; 6 Outlet Connection Pipe; 7 Lower Radiator Tank; 8 Radiator Tubing and Fins; 9 Fan; 10 Upper Radiator Tank; 11 Fill Here; 12 Motor Exhaust Pipe.

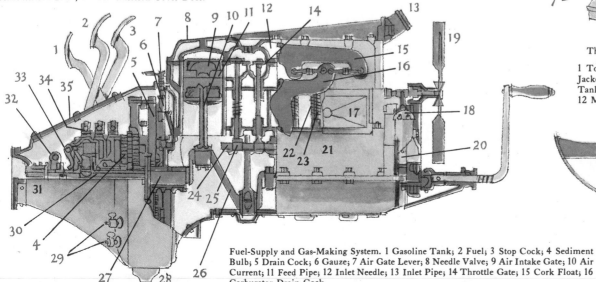

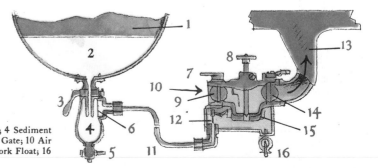

Fuel-Supply and Gas-Making System. 1 Gasoline Tank; 2 Fuel; 3 Stop Cock; 4 Sediment Bulb; 5 Drain Cock; 6 Gauze; 7 Air Gate Lever; 8 Needle Valve; 9 Air Intake Gate; 10 Air Current; 11 Feed Pipe; 12 Inlet Needle; 13 Inlet Pipe; 14 Throttle Gate; 15 Cork Float; 16 Carburetor Drain Cock.